Poppy's Party

Written by Julie Ward & Illustrated by Joan Paar

From Grandma Cookie,
Many happy
"Surprises"
Julie Ward

For those who like surprises

Poppy's Party

Written by Julie Ward
Illustrated by Joan Paar
Creative Design by Ella Reid

The Real Flowers of Happy Flower Island

 Poppy Poppies are known to be brightly colored.

 Daisy Their petals open as the sun comes up and close at night.

 Marigold A smelly flower that deters some insects.

 Magnolia The magnolia grows on a tree and is common in the southern United States.

 Rose Well known for its scent, it can be used in perfumes.

 Dandelion A pretty yellow flower that is thought of as a weed.

 Peony This flower blooms in late Spring and can live up to 100 years.

Poppy popped out of bed ready for her big day.

Birthdays are a BIG deal on Happy Flower Island.

She checked her red petals in the mirror, then opened the front

door **excited** to hear all the birthday wishes from her friends.

"Here I am!" she said as she stepped outside.

No one was there.

Not a single friend had come to wish

her a Happy Birthday.

There was not even a gift on her doorstep.

"They couldn't have forgotten my birthday, could they?"

Across the garden at Mari Gold's, her honeybee alarm woke her bright and early.

Buzz buzz

"Poppy's party is going to be a perfect surprise." She smiled and thought of the fun day the flowers were planning.

Peter Pigeon flew through the window and

dropped a message on her bedspread.

5

Mari Gold giggled thinking of the angry butterfly.

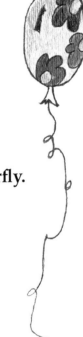

At Rose Thornson's house, the smell

of baking filled the air.

Ding   Rose was so excited about the cake

she forgot to use oven mitts.

"Ouch!" Rose cried. The cake dropped to the floor.

"Everyone is counting on cake and my hands

hurt," she cried running cold water over

her drooping flower petals.

"I guess I will have to go to Magnolia's

Market for more ingredients."

Poppy was walking
down the path when Rose
Thornson *scurried* past her.

"Hi Rose! It's a lovely day today," said Poppy.

"Yes, you too," said Rose bustling by.

Poppy was confused. Rose didn't make any sense.

"Oh well, maybe she is having a *bad* day,"
thought Poppy.

Pink Peony was
sewing a quilt
for Poppy.

She was thirsty from working very hard.
She lifted her glass of juice just as
Mrs. Daisy **knocked** on the door.

Startled, she *spilled* all over the quilt.

"Oh no, this must be washed."

"I'm going to Magnolia's Market," said
Mrs. Daisy as she popped her head into
Pink Peony's door. "She sells Soapy Suds."

Pink Peony and Mrs. Daisy entered Magnolia's Market.

They saw Poppy by the fruit.

"Oh jeepers," said Mrs. Daisy. "I hope

she leaves soon. She is standing where I

need to be. I do not want Poppy to wonder

why I am buying so much food.

She might suspect we are

going to have a party."

"We are," giggled Pink Peony.

Mrs. Daisy saw a display with sunglasses and beach hats.

She grabbed a pair of sunglasses, a beach hat and a basket.

"She won't recognize me now," said Mrs. Daisy.

She walked right up to Poppy.

"It sure is a nice day," said Mrs. Daisy in a funny voice.

"Yes it is. You must be new here. I'm Poppy,"

said Poppy. "What is your name?"

"I'm Dandelion," said Mrs. Daisy.

"Today is my birthday," said Poppy.

"Would you like to celebrate it with me?"

"I can't today. I am making a fruit salad," said Mrs.

Daisy, still disguised as Dandelion.

"I can help," said Poppy.

"No thank you, this I must do alone," Mrs. Daisy

continued in her silly tone.

"Well, have a good day," said Poppy.

Poppy was sad, but determined she would have a happy birthday with her friends or without. She placed a strawberry cupcake with vanilla frosting in her basket. She also chose a candle and a streamer with "Happy Birthday" written on it.

Poppy walked up to the front counter. Magnolia felt bad for her friend, but she did not want to ruin the surprise.

"Nice day today, isn't it? Do you have any plans?" Magnolia asked Poppy as she placed the cupcake in a bag.

"Just eating a cupcake," said Poppy.

Poppy was surprised that Magnolia did not notice what she was buying.

"That sounds nice," said Magnolia.

Just then Danny Dragon walked into the store.

"You be careful now Danny!" said Magnolia.

"I was looking for Mari Gold.

Oh Poppy what are you doing here on your..."

"Hi Danny!" shouted Mari Gold.

"Oh, there you are," Danny said as

he shuffled over to Mari Gold.

"That was a close call," thought Mari Gold.

Poppy went
home and set
the cupcake
on a plate.

She did not want to feel sad, but she did. How could her

friends forget her birthday?

There was a **knock** on her door.

It was Mrs. Daisy.

"You must come to Pink Peony's right away."

"Is she okay?" Poppy said as she forgot all about her birthday.

"Oh yes," said Mrs. Daisy. "She wants to have a word with you."

Poppy and Mrs. Daisy walked down the garden path.

Poppy wondered if everything was all right.

Had she said something to upset Pink Peony?

When they got to Pink Peony's house all looked quiet.

"Is she even home?" asked Poppy.

She knocked on the door, no answer. She knocked again.

"I think you should just go in Poppy.

She asked to see you," said Mrs. Daisy.

Slowly she opened the door

"Hello. Is anyone here?"

"SURPRISE!"

all the flowers shouted together.

Poppy jumped and then cheered, "You didn't
forget my birthday! Yippee!"

"We *never* forget a birthday on Happy
Flower Island," said Mari Gold.

All were celebrating when a butterfly
flew into the room, straight up
Danny's nose.

"Ahh, Ahhh…"

The butterfly shot out of Danny's nose.

He did not sneeze.

"*Phew*," the flowers sighed with relief.

The flowers had fun playing games like pin
the tail on the dragon, bobbing for apples,
and ring around the Rosie.

They hit a piñata full of tasty treats.
They ate fruit salad and cake for dessert and
had fun because they were together.

The flowers felt sad that Poppy
thought she was
forgotten and made a promise
to each other to always tell the
truth if they felt sad.

The End

About the Author

Julie Ward lives in Fort Myers, Florida,
with her husband, son and black lab, Foxxy.

About the Illustrator

Joan Paar lives with her husband in rural
Grantsburg, Wisconsin. They see lots of wild animals,
but no dragons.

Made in the USA
Columbia, SC
13 April 2019